The Trapeze Diaries

Marie Carter

D1521713

Hanging Loose Press
Brooklyn, New York

Published by Hanging Loose Press, 231 Wyckoff Street, Brooklyn, NY, 11217. All rights reserved. No part of this book may be reproduced without the publisher's written permission, except for brief quotations in reviews.

Printed in the United States of America

10 9 8 7 6 5 4 3 2 1

Hanging Loose Press thanks the Literature Program of the New York State Council on the Arts for a grant in support of the publication of this book.

Author's note: Although this narrative has some basis in the author's experiences, several characters are composites and names have been changed. Therefore, this book should be classified fiction, and it is the author's hope to convey an emotional truth rather than a factual one.

Cover photograph by Maike Schultz
Cover design by Marie Carter

Library of Congress Cataloging-in-Publication Data available on request.

ISBN: 978-1-931236-84-3 (pbk)
ISBN: 978-1-931236-85-0 (cloth)

 Produced at The Print Center, Inc. 225 Varick St., New York, NY 10014, a non-profit facility for literary and arts-related publications. (212) 206-8465

To

Natalie Agee

I Wang

Shell Fischer

Taniya Sen

"The reason why people love to engage in dangerous activities...although they may not be aware of it, is that it forces them into the Now—that intensely alive state that is free of time, free of problems, free of thinking, free of the burden of personality. Slipping away from the present moment even for a second may mean death."

The Power of Now by Eckhart Tolle

"However solid things may appear on the surface, everything in life is changing, without exception. Even Mount Everest—the perfect symbol of indomitable, unyielding, massively solid reality—is 'growing' a quarter of an inch a year...."

Faith by Sharon Salzberg

"It rained a lot this year
And again it rains today
Perhaps this evening you will not have time
But as for me I go to sleep surrounded by many images
Which remind me that I'm still thinking of you.
Goodnight Papa."

Cirque Éloize's *Rain*

The Aerialist caught the hoop beautifully every time, sometimes with her feet, sometimes with her arms, sometimes with her ankles, once with her head. She projected long shadows against the wall of the tent. Many times I thought she might fall and break her neck, but she didn't. It was the first time I'd seen anything like it. From a distance, she looked perfect. She did not seem to sweat. She did not seem to breathe. Her body appeared weightless. She was so far above me she could have been an angel.

Later, I couldn't stop thinking about her. I was so touched by the way she defied everything human in herself: unafraid of heights, flexible and strong.

That night, I dreamt shadows were dancing above me. I thought I was falling from a trapeze and I woke to my own shuddering.

The older I get the more aware I become of my own mortality: A colleague of mine recently lost his life to pancreatic cancer, and four years ago my father died, suddenly, of a heart attack.

When I take the bus home at night, I fall asleep and dream the bus crashes and I break my arm and crush my hip. I've been thinking about Edward Abbey's words in *Desert Solitaire*: "The fear of death follows from the fear of life. A man who lives fully is prepared to die at any time."

After I saw the Aerialist perform I bought souvenirs: a CD, a T-shirt, and a pen, but when I got home realized it wasn't enough. There was something else I wanted, something not quite tangible that I had left behind. And for weeks after the circus I walked around with this feeling.

During my lunch break in the summer, I walk to the West Side Highway to watch people taking lessons at the flying trapeze school. I feel envious as strong flexible men and women fly through the air and hang upside down by their knees. Then they roll off the net, faces red with exhilaration.

My friend, Christa, and I met at a writing workshop several years ago. When she was younger she'd been a gymnast, starting at the age of six. She gave it up as a teenager because she was so good at it that the other kids hated her for running off with all the trophies. I tell her I've been thinking about studying trapeze. She urges me to do so while I'm still young. She's now in her forties.

Christa asks if I believe in the afterlife.

"I'm not sure what I believe," I say. "I'm agnostic."

She nods. "It's a shame you're not religious, and I'm not suggesting you should be," she says, "but some people find it a helpful tool in coping with death."

"My father was agnostic, too," I say.

My father was a quiet man. He often disguised his feelings through humor. I feel cheated by his death. I hadn't really gotten to know him. I do remember that he was a perfectionist. He was always fixing tiny anomalies and straightening pictures around the house.

After I left home, on occasional visits to my parents, I would go around the house late at night making all the pictures crooked, as a prank. When my father woke, I would hear him yelp at the bottom of the stairs. Several hours later, he'd still be straightening the frames on the wall.

At the local bookstore I come across a book called *Your Loved One Lives on Within You*. I pick it up.

The book talks about using your imagination to sustain a relationship with someone you love who has died. "It is true that . . . you will never again be in the physical presence of the person. However . . . an inner relationship . . . continues on after death."

Very early in the morning, I see my father sitting on the edge of my bed, examining the pictures on my wall. He squints at them and points.

"That one's crooked," he says, getting up from the bed to set it right again.

I say nothing. I had followed Christa's advice and signed up for fixed trapeze class. Now I've barely slept all night in anticipation of my first lesson.

My father continues to observe the room and adjust things: the cracked plaster on my wall, the wobbly chair, the doorknob that comes apart in my hands.

I curl back under the covers and nap. When I wake again to check my watch, it is five-thirty. My father is wiping at the dirty marks on my blinds.

Waiting for the Aerialist's trapeze partner, Rich, to bring me the forms, I gaze around the studio. The walls are exposed brick; the sprung wood floors are lined with mats. In a far corner of the room, trapezes, hoops, batons, and other circus props occupy an open attic space. My father inspects them, tutting at small cracks in the batons, and the hoops wound with tape not quite aligned to his taste.

I fill out the forms, pausing over the emergency number section. With all my family in Scotland, I don't know who I should put down as an emergency contact. Someone like Christa? Or my boss? What if I fall off the trapeze and break my neck? Who would be the most useful person to contact? Would they mind being contacted?

Signing the release form, all I can see are the words "accident" and "death."

The class is doing handstands against the wall; each student with hands pressed down on the floor and one leg in the air, kicking upward. Even when I was a child and supposedly more flexible, I couldn't do handstands. I've never done anything like this. I walk my feet up the wall and try to bring my hands in but they stay a good two feet away. My arms are in agony.

I am in this L-shaped position when the Aerialist walks in. Her pageboy, Louise Brooks-style haircut looks like someone has set a bowl on her head and chopped around it. Her hazel eyes are large, like Amelie's in the French movie. She has broad shoulders, and up close her arms are larger than I remembered and muscular. Blue veins protrude from her arms like thick wires. Her forearms are almost as thick as her upper arms; her fingers are long and thin like a pianist's. In the show she was all spangles and glitter, but in class she is wearing a frayed T-shirt and tracksuit bottoms with holes in them.

"Sorry I'm late," she says to Rich, who is warming us up. She sees me watching her from my upside down position and smiles. My cheeks flush. I'm the only one who had to walk into the handstand. I feel foolish.

My father, watching me from the corner of the room, picks nervously at the skin around his fingernails.

The Aerialist is putting up a trapeze. The bar at the bottom, five feet off the ground, resembles a toilet roll tube, but thicker. Suspended from the ceiling are two climbing ropes stitched with red velvet, one attached to each side of the bar. The ceiling is about 12 feet high; from a standing position, I could hit the bar with my forehead. Someone told me once that the fixed trapeze, hanging low to the ground, is less frightening than the flying trapeze for those who suffer from fear of heights, but it takes more strength because you can't use momentum.

The Aerialist is wrapping the trapeze bar in adhesive tape. She puts gauze on top of the bar so the tape won't stick to our hands. It looks like a wounded arm.

I envy and admire the Aerialist. She can do so many things I can't: splits all the way down, both thighs touching the ground; freestanding handstands and headstands. She can arch her back so far doing knee beats that she can wrap her arms around her legs. She jumps through hoops and lands in a forward roll.

In the photograph of the Aerialist at the studio, she is smirking boldly at the camera. She looks mischievous, open, frank and gorgeous. She is everything I want but am scared to be.

"Circus people make this look so damn easy," the Aerialist says, pointing at the trapeze. "But it takes so much patience and it hurts like hell. You're probably going to cry; you'll get angry and frustrated. You'll definitely bruise and most likely you'll get scared. Obviously we don't want any serious injuries, but it's good for you to challenge yourself. Let fear teach you; it's good to have a healthy amount of fear."

When I saw her performing she moved so lyrically on a trapeze that I would have expected her voice to be soft and gentle, but it isn't. It's harsh and full of experience. It's a husky voice, gravelly like a jazz singer's.

As she talks I notice peanut butter stuck between her teeth.

The Aerialist decides we should work on Bird's Nest, one of the simplest tricks. I take my turn: Upside down, my hands holding the bar and my knees hooked over it, I slide my legs up the rope then curl and arch my back, turning under to face the other side of the room, hanging from the bar as if about to dive into a pool. This seems like it should be easy to do, but it takes several tries for me to get it, and other students are watching, so I have a hard time focusing on the movement. I feel embarrassed, scared and self-conscious. This was a stupid idea, I tell myself, since I'm scared of heights and of being upside down.

Meghan, a yoga instructor, is next. Her arms are thin but toned; as she hangs upside down, her tightly pulled-in abdominal muscles are revealed under her T-shirt. She nails Bird's Nest on her first try. Meghan is destined to be a trapeze artist; I am not.

And yet, after my first trapeze lesson ends, I can barely stop smiling. It is a sweltering summer evening, not quite dark yet, and the sun is still out. People on the subway look at me oddly. I am glowing and my hands are shaking. It's the hardest and most humiliating thing I've ever done, but somehow I am in love. Watching the others run through the trick, and being on the bar myself, I had been constantly in awe, as though the trapeze were a divine thing.

Meghan, the yoga instructor, asks if I want to join her class. "Trapeze is hard," she says. "It would be good for you to get some other kind of training on the side."

I've never felt comfortable in gyms. I wouldn't know how to operate the equipment and I don't fit in with the gym aesthetic. But I thought I could try yoga. It seemed gentle, and I've known people studying it who have varying physical abilities. I had not, however, thought there would be a spiritual component to the class.

"What is left behind when you die?" Meghan asks as we transition from Downward-Facing Dog to Plank. "Not the body, but how people remember you. If you want to be remembered well, while you're still alive, be a creature of love."

Later, I position myself in a shoulder stand but my arms are too wide apart and far from my back.

"If you come to yoga, you must be looking for some kind of change. What is the transformation you want?" Meghan asks.

She clamps her hands around my feet and kicks my elbows inwards. I yelp because my back is sore and, rather than helping, this exercise hurts.

Meghan gives me a puzzled look. "I'm not going to let you go," she says, perhaps annoyed that I won't trust her.

My father appears at my side and whispers, "Relax," so I do, but the pain is intense and I'm afraid I won't be able to get back down.

I keep searching for reasons why I'm so afraid. Is it because when I was three my mother let me slide and fall over on the ice without holding me up? Is it that when I was six-years-old I fell and hit my mouth on a metal table, cut my gums and had to get them stitched? Or is it because of my father's death?

Everybody has these memories of physical traumas, so why is my fear particularly debilitating?

I have read that it is less useful to know where these feelings come from than how to deal with them when they arise.

Meghan lets my legs go and my father whispers, "Good work."

I am becoming aware that I trust my father's ghost to hold me up more than I trust a real person.

I don't know why I find hanging from my knees so difficult.

The Aerialist says, "Open up here," and she pokes my abdominal muscles with her index finger. "I've got your feet; you won't fall," she says, but I don't believe her.

And I can't open up. Something in my belly is clenching.

One Saturday morning my best friend, Jen, and I were supposed to visit my parents. It was 11:30—I was expecting Jen about noon—when I got a frantic call from my brother: my father had had a heart attack and was being taken to the hospital. I should get there right away. Jen came to my house immediately; within ten minutes of the call we were speeding down the highway. We had to stop for gas. I went to a phone box to call my mother. "I think," my mother said, "he's gone already."

We couldn't believe what was happening. At a medical checkup a month earlier the doctor had said my dad was in perfect health.

They kept him on a respirator but he made no progress. We visited every day for four long days. My mother kept threatening, "If he goes, I go." She said it so decidedly that my brother and I believed her.

"Even if he came back to life," the doctor said gently, "and that's doubtful, he would be severely brain damaged. He probably wouldn't recognize any of you."

After a family discussion we unanimously agreed to ask the doctor to turn off the machine.

I wanted time alone with my dad, but doctors, nurses, and other visitors were buzzing around the bed.

I bent close to his face and whispered, "I love you so much." My fingers traced the shape of the liver spots on his hands. His mouth hung open. He said nothing.

A thirteen-year-old student fell from the bar. She wasn't doing any funky moves when she fell; she was in a Pike, hands on the bar, body folded beneath. She lost her grip and crashed onto the mat. She had, at least, the good sense to tuck her head in as she fell. She wasn't terribly hurt but she was embarrassed and in shock. She lay on the mat crying for half an hour until her mother came to pick her up. The Aerialist stayed with her until then, soothing her, telling her not to apologize and saying that she did the right thing by tucking her head under.

A week later, the Aerialist assured us the student had no injury. "Adults are different from children," she said. "They have this mental system they can check into, but kids think they can do everything." I wish I could remember being like that as a child, but I had been the opposite. I was fearful and cautious.

I have always been scared of heights. I have an early memory (maybe I was five) of climbing the stairs at St. Paul's Cathedral in London with my parents and brother. My father was having trouble with his hip at the time and only got part way up the stairs. He was walking with a stick. He was also afraid of heights. I remember my mother taking hold of my hand and pulling me out of the stairwell and onto the balcony of St. Paul's. I had recently seen a horror movie about a woman who had jumped from the roof of the building.

"Why is the woman screaming?" I had asked my mum.

"What happens to her when she falls?"

"She dies," my mother had said.

At Saint Paul's Cathedral, my mother gestured with her hands and said, "Look at the lovely view," but I was too scared to admire it. I walked around the circular dome with my back pressed hard against the wall, not daring to look down. I didn't want to die. My mother and brother leaned over the edge.

I was not an adventurous kid. One day, when I was ten-years-old, it was snowing and my mother said she wanted to get me out of the house. She was tired of me nesting in my room, reading a book. She decided she would take me sledding the next day on a small hill near the back of our house where other children went sledding, threw snowballs and made snowmen.

The night before we went sledding, I had nightmares. In one dream, I lost a leg. In another, I died in a sledding accident. I couldn't envision how the experience of sledding might turn out well. I was incredibly nervous on my first day but, once I got into it, I stopped worrying. I even became quite adept at it when I lost my fear. But still, I was always cautious about everything. From flying in an airplane to roller skating to riding my bike to camping, I always lived in fear of something new.

I always believed I would fail.

I'm worried it's not possible for me to change. Some scientists think we're born with our personalities, that they're ingrained in our genes. Accepting this comforts me because now I don't have to worry about taking responsibility for my destiny or trying to change myself. But I worry about my ability to do trapeze. I'm worried that I'll always be scared, that my possibilities are severely limited.

I go to see a show called *Circo Commedia*. One half of the performing duet is said to have ridden a unicycle from the age of eleven, beginning when he used it on his paper route.

His circus abilities must have been genetically ingrained. I am envious that he realized them at such a young age.

I have been reading articles about the circus that say Americans don't train circus artists early enough. They are talking about people who start training at eighteen. I am twenty-six years old.

I keep thinking of the Colorado man I read about in *Outside* magazine. When he was twenty-one, his friends knew him as a taco-eating pig. When one of them took him to the gym, he could barely do two squats. Now he's become one of the toughest, most disciplined instructors of iron yoga and bodybuilding in the state.

This man gives me faith. If a taco-eating pig can do what he's done, then I can become an aerialist.

A few days after my first class I am at dinner with Christa and her husband in their apartment. During our conversation, I tell her I can't do handstands. As a former gymnast, she decides to teach me this basic trick by spotting me into a handstand against the wall. That is, she stands close to catch me in case I land badly.

I tumble into a half-assed handstand and feel myself instantly falling back down when Christa grabs my legs and sends me back up. There's a shaking sensation in my arms, blood rushes to my head and I feel disoriented. I let out a little yelp, more from fear than pain. My legs pivot back down to the floor so I'm upright.

"You did it," she says, smiling.

"Even when I was a kid, I couldn't do it," I tell her.

Now that I am able to go back up with help, I need to learn to do it by myself.

Christa spots me four more times. On the fifth try, she pulls away from me.

"Try it on your own now," she says.

So I try by myself. To my surprise, my whole body tumbles over into this strong, upside-down shape, my feet pressed against the wall.

The ad on TV for a fitness center is captioned, "The Power to Amaze Yourself."

After my father died my mother looked up to me as though I were a big sister who would take care of her and show her what to do. I often worried about how she would cope after I left Scotland.

For the first three months I would take her out with my friends on weekends. The first time, we went to a bar and everyone bought drinks in rounds. When it came to my mother's turn, she handed me money and said, "You get this."

"Why?" I said. "We're all taking turns getting rounds."

"I've never ordered a drink at the bar by myself, at least not since I was twenty. I don't know what to do," she said.

Eventually I persuaded her to order drinks by herself. She seemed nervous, but she did okay and later she felt proud of herself.

After my father's death, my mother frequently expressed anxieties about living on just her income.

"How do you do it?" she asked me one night. "You don't make a lot of money and yet you manage."

"But I share an apartment," I said, "and I don't own a house or a car."

Just before I went to the U.S., my mother kept giving me money. Every time we met, she would slip a twenty in my hand, and would insist on paying for lunch.

"I won't be able to treat you much longer," she would say. She equated moving to a foreign country with death.

My father had died at a point in my life when I was in a flurry of activity. I had exams to pass, money to earn, a U.S. visa to apply for, packing to do and an internship to complete. It wasn't difficult for me to occupy all of my time. I was determined not to cry in front of anyone, my mother included. I wanted to appear strong. I didn't want to upset anyone and I didn't want grief to take up my time.

Several months after my father's death I graduated from college and moved to New York. Then the grief and sadness mounted. Sometimes on the subway I'd cry for no apparent reason while people looked the other way. Often I'd arrive home after an ordinary day and find myself sobbing in the bath.

I hadn't realized that grief could take so long.

On her first visit to New York, my mother asked, "Do you ever think about your dad?" and I wanted to tell her, "All the time," but I didn't.

On September 11th I watched the people jumping from the Twin Towers. At first it looked like large pieces of rubble and debris falling down but when I borrowed someone's binoculars, I could see people were tumbling like acrobats off the edges of the buildings. All the office workers were out on their roofs gawking.

My mother was frantic—she knew I worked in downtown Manhattan but she had no idea of the actual size of the area. She was sure I had been killed until she received an email from me assuring her otherwise.

A few months later she visited me in New York, and from the Brooklyn Bridge I showed her the enormity of what is considered downtown Manhattan. Relief came over her face.

Shortly after that, my mother was diagnosed with M.S. Her symptoms had become more prominent after my father's death. She would often lose her balance and have difficulty walking. For the whole year before she was diagnosed, the doctor, telling her it was "just grief," had been prescribing anti-depressants and sleeping pills. The hospital staff continually set her up with appointments for scans, then sent her for the wrong ones.

When my mother first learned she had M.S. she was full of fear, saying things like, "I could go blind," or "Next year I could be in a wheelchair."

Now, every time I have to meet her on a street corner, I worry even if she is only five minutes late. I imagine her passed out on the sidewalk somewhere or falling on the subway stairs. But she always turns up each time, smiling.

There is a poster for a missing old lady in the window of the pastry shop in Bensonhurst where I live. I wonder where in New York one might find a missing old lady.

A year before his death, my father had a hip replacement. He seemed to recover pretty well. At one point, he was walking five miles a day. He kept busy with the jigsaw puzzles I gave him and started to build model airplanes.

"Your father wasn't very patient with illness," my mother says. "He didn't like it when I was ill. He'd get cross and tell me I was imagining things."

When my mother was diagnosed, I started looking at my own body for signs of decay. M.S. can be inherited. Sometimes I would imagine little pockets of foreign bodies lying dormant in my organs, ready to awaken and destroy me.

On her most recent visit to New York, my mother found it hard to walk and had to be met at the airport with a wheelchair. I can't stand the thought of leaving my home in New York and going back to Scotland, yet I feel enormous guilt about not being there for her. Every time she leaves New York, I think this will be the last time I will see her because she is sure to die soon, just like my father. Sometimes I panic and have difficulty breathing. I spend the last few days of her visit crying, and can't seem to stop, even when I'm at work. I am so embarrassed I have to keep running to the bathroom to calm down.

My mother's father died when she was ten years old. His death has profoundly affected her throughout her life. When I lived with my parents, she would never let me leave the house after we'd had an argument without hugging me. "You never know," she'd say, "when one of us could drop dead."

One night, several years ago, on my way home to Brooklyn, I was almost raped. The man didn't have any weapons but I was scared to hit him in case he retaliated. Instead, I struggled to run away and screamed until a car stopped and the couple inside came out and scared him off.

At that point I began losing all sense of trust in strangers. If someone asked me for the time, I would move a foot away before looking at my watch.

Someone in a coffee shop is asking me, "If you fell from the trapeze, what height would you be falling from?"

"Only about five feet," I tell him, "Plus I have a classmate or teacher as a spot and there are mats underneath the bar."

This is something of bravado on my part. It is still possible, even with those safeguards in place, for terrible accidents to occur. Part of me has to retain an enormous amount of faith that nothing bad will happen.

Professional trapeze artist Juan Vazquez says, "Every time I go up I ask the Lord to help my brother and my daughter, and I have an angel that protects us."

On the other hand, since I have started trapeze I have become more aware of the numerous dangers that challenge all of us every day. I wanted to ask the man in the coffee shop, "When you cross the road, how do you know a car won't run the red light?" It's those moments when we are being mindless that accidents can happen. When I practice trapeze, I am extremely careful about what I'm doing; I pay more attention to what is happening around me than I do going about my daily life.

The other day I watched a large man rushing so hard out of the train that he knocked another man, who was taking a simple walk, off his feet. The man lay on the floor unconscious until an ambulance came to collect him.

About a year after I was almost raped, I was walking by myself at Coney Island when a kid came up behind me, stuck a knife in my back and said, "Yo, bitch. Give me your money." The sky was gray, it was early winter and it looked like it was going to rain. There were several other kids lurking about ten feet away, probably his friends, waiting to offer assistance if I didn't comply.

"Is that everything?" the kid said, after I had emptied my wallet of everything but my credit cards.

"Yeah," I said, praying he would leave me alone.

I broke into a run then stopped a couple strolling on the beach and asked them to walk with me to the subway. I didn't want to be on my own anymore.

My father trailed behind us, a concerned look on his face.

They were Russian. I told them I'm from Scotland.

"Do you like living in New York?" they asked.

"Not today," I said, and laughed out of a sense of relief.

"Why do you walk alone?" the woman asked. "You should have someone come with you."

Perhaps I am more of a target when I am on my own, but even when people are in groups of two or three, when someone points a knife or a gun, the numbers don't matter anymore.

"I'm a writer," I said, as though that explained everything.

"I understand," the woman said.

"Go home," she said when we reached the subway, "and call someone, okay? And don't go walking by yourself anymore."

I nodded half-heartedly.

The Aerialist says, "The only way to conquer fear after a fall is to repeatedly do the trick again."

The Aerialist is trying to position me into an Ankle Hang, where I would be upside down, gripping the outside of the ropes with my ankles and the inside of the ropes with my calves, but my feet keep sliding and I get nervous. My head inches toward the floor.

"Ouch!" I say feeling the rope burn into my ankles.

"Hurts, doesn't it?" the Aerialist says, teasingly. "Now open up here." Her hands touch my hips and then she runs the tip of her finger down the length of my thigh. I am in pain and also being turned on.

After a couple of seconds I can't take the pain anymore so I sit back up and take hold of the bar with my hands, push my legs into Knee Hang, then take my feet off the bar, one at a time.

"Nice," the Aerialist says.

But for me, it is not enough.

"Sorry," I say to her.

"Don't apologize to me," she says.

Later, I realize I am apologizing to myself.

After my father died, I tried to find ways to help my mother occupy her time. I introduced her to a friend of mine in her fifties who was studying literature at college. I wanted my mother to know such things were possible at her age.

"But I'm not that bright," my mother kept insisting. "I was always getting poor grades in high school." Her teachers had persistently told her what a stupid child she was, but I don't buy it. I think that, in spite of what she says, my mother is terribly smart.

I have my doubts that I can get good at trapeze. I'm stuck in the memory of the past when I was a high school girl and always the last in school races or the last to get picked for hockey teams. I wasn't interested in sports. All I wanted to do was read books.

In yoga class, Meghan says, "Watch out for those negative thoughts. If you keep telling yourself you can't do something, your body will give you exactly what you want."

Sometimes I try to learn from my mother. The Aerialist is spotting me for One-Knee Hang now that I am able to do Knee Hang by myself but I've been clinging to this image of myself as weak and incapable of meeting such a physical challenge. To myself I admit my resemblance to my mother— I am more faithful to the story of the past than to the one unfolding in front of me.

People often comment on the fact that I've lost my accent. "Both my parents were English, but I grew up in Scotland," I often explain, "so I have a chameleonlike accent that changes according to its environment."

But it's more than that. What I often don't say is that the

31

purging of my accent is also a kind of purging of the past. I changed the color of my hair four times within a year of arriving in New York. At one point, I dyed it blonde but it ended up looking green. I got my nose pierced and my hair cut drastically short, cropped so close to my head I could have been mistaken for a Buddhist monk or a thug. I hoped that when my mother came to visit, she wouldn't be able to recognize me.

I come from a small town where it is unusual for people to leave home. Most parents and grandparents still have their children around to look after them. When I talk to people from my hometown, there's a certain amount of accusation in their voices.

Christa tells me I am helping my mother by being happy.

At night I like to work out; I do backbends, hold handstands for a minute followed by splits. When my mother comes to visit she watches, grimacing.

"Don't do that," she keeps saying. "You'll hurt yourself."

The more she tells me not to do the exercises, the more extreme I want to make them. I remember with some resentment how she mollycoddled me when I was a child.

People in my trapeze class joke that they resent their parents for not sending them to circus school when they were younger. Sometimes I have the absurd desire to grab young children by the shoulders and yell, "Train with the circus while you're still young!"

My mother is full of more questions than I can answer. *What time do you have lunch? Who do you have lunch with? Where do you have lunch? Do you go out most evenings or do you stay in? Do you always wear black socks? Do you ever wear jewelry?* I'd like to draw her some graphs, have someone set up a study.

People are always telling I'm a patient person, but they are wrong.

"You're so patient with yourself," the Aerialist tells me.

But at night when I get home, I tend to beat myself up.

"I'm still not able to get up to the bar with both my legs simultaneously. I still kick up and pivot using one leg at a time," I complain to Christa. "All the other people in the class are learning these advanced tricks. It's taking so long."

When I look behind me I notice my father is attempting, to no avail, to touch his toes over his large belly. He stands up, looks at me and says, "That's my exercise for the day, then."

I tell Christa that my life is in a rut and that I don't feel like I'm progressing.

"Things are happening for you," she says, and reels off a list of things I've done in the last year. "They're just not happening as fast as you want them to."

The Aerialist is showing off in a one-armed handstand without using the wall or a spot. We shake our heads in amazement.

"It only took nineteen years of practice," she jokes.

When I was little, my family and neighbors used to play dress up. I was always the fairy princess, my brother the handsome prince and my father humored us by playing the ugly wizard who cackled in the corner and disrupted everyone's happiness with his evil spells.

"Don't you think I should be over my father's death by now?" I ask Christa.

She shrugs, watching me carefully. My father is sitting next to me sleeping, his head resting on my shoulder. When I was growing up he was a fervent nap-taker. I'd often find him on the couch with his mouth hanging open, snoring. My mother used to say he was so laid back he was falling over.

"It sounds like you didn't deal with your father's death at the time it happened," Christa is saying. "You've been holding on to your grief for a long while."

"I'm ashamed to cry in front of other people," I confess.

"Everyone is too embarrassed to cry in public," Christa says.

Every year around the anniversary of my father's death, I look for and find things that remind me of and bring me closer to him: an old man with a wooden walking stick, a can of peaches, milk in a jam jar, a man choking on cigarette smoke, a bagpiper in Union Square playing "Scotland the Brave." Several days after his death, my mother had said in a haunted voice, "I keep looking for him everywhere," and several years later I find myself doing the same thing.

In Cirque du Soleil's documentary, *Fire Within,* Olga Pikhienko's father is coaching his daughter for a lead role.

His daughter moans that she is not getting enough time to rehearse on the stage and that she's forgetting some of her choreography. She's scared she'll be a failure on opening night.

"We'll just have to do what we can," he says sternly, as her coach, but as her father he looks tearful.

I am watching Charlie Chaplin's *The Circus*, while my father sits in his favorite rocking chair chortling loudly and slapping his thighs.

When I was a child and my father took me to the cinema, I was always embarrassed, because people would laugh at him laughing. In all the photographs I have of my father, he is pulling a funny face. He didn't like to be serious.

At the beginning of *The Circus*, a trapeze artist is swinging from the rafters. After the show, her father slaps her across the face and chastises her for a poor performance while she begs him for mercy. She was "trying."

I am practicing handstands, belly to the wall. I have been trying to hold them for a minute then walk my hands back out. Instead, my legs tend to fall over in the opposite direction, my back curving into an arch. When I fall to the ground with a nasty thump, my father collapses laughing.

My father didn't like to express affection in words, but with actions.

When I was a little girl, I'd sometimes be sitting on the couch watching television; my father would kneel in front of me and hand me a comb from his back pocket.

"Comb my hair," he'd say.

Sometimes, he let me decorate his hair with bows and ribbons.

For the past few mornings I've woken up with a tingling sensation in my hands. My fingers tend to cramp when I'm working at a keyboard. Looking up my symptoms on line, I find out I might have carpal tunnel syndrome from continual strain on my wrists.

When I see the neurologist for a test she tells me the needle will hurt.

"Are you chicken or are you quite good with pain?" she asks.

"Chicken," I say. My father is in the corner of the room inspecting equipment, adjusting control panels. I half expect everything to blow up.

The neurologist tells me that she'll be gentle and that I can look the other way if that will make it easier.

She inserts the needle and I don't even flinch.

After the test is over, she says, "You're not chicken at all. You didn't even say a word. I had a police officer in here earlier who did the same test and he was screaming."

The Aerialist is trying to teach me Skin-the-Cat. From pike position, I am supposed to lower my feet to the ground so my shoulders and upper arms twist. Once my feet hit the ground, I must release my grip from the bar to stand. I look at the Aerialist, horrified: I know I can't do this. I don't think I'll be able to hold my weight. It looks painful on the shoulders.

I don't like the way they twist.

"Try it on a lower bar," she suggests.

Out of the corner of my eye I spot my father who is attempting to hula-hoop. He tries to get his protruding belly to catch the edge of the hoop, but he drops it every time. I feel nervous for his hip, a constant source of irritation to him, until I remember that he's not alive.

I go to the lower bar as the Aerialist suggests but I'm still afraid. I push myself to do it though, and I'm amazed to find it doesn't hurt at all. In fact, it's surprisingly easy. I am learning that the fear of pain is much worse than pain itself.

Someone in class is talking about the time she took a flying trapeze class and knocked heads with her catcher. "We were both out, unconscious for several minutes," she says. "But they made me get back out there and throw the same trick with the catcher again. I had a black eye and I had to get up at ten the next day for another class. When I threw the trick again, I could barely let go of the bar."

The Aerialist remembers when she began learning a swinging trapeze routine. "I used to black out from fear," she says.

I have heard of trapeze artists having serious accidents on the fixed trapeze as well: everything from a black eye to death. So far, all I've gotten are some nasty bruises on my arms. I am waiting for the worst to happen.

The Aerialist tells me, "I keep chipping my teeth."

Christa has been nagging me to teach her trapeze.

"I just want to try it. It looks like so much fun. It reminds me of the bar when I was a gymnast."

I rent the studio from the Aerialist so I can show Christa some tricks. I am excited about teaching a gymnast. I am sure she will pick it up in no time. When we are in yoga class together, Christa can do all the complicated poses and transitions: Crow to Plank, forearm stand without a wall, headstand in full Lotus.

But as soon as Christa gets on the trapeze bar, she yelps with pain.

I show her Angels 1, 2, 3, & 4; Bird's Nest; Knee Hang; Sitting to Standing.

"This hurts so much," Christa complains. "Why do you torture yourself like this? Are you a masochist or something?"

"Only on the weekends," I joke.

After ten minutes she comes down. "I am not getting on that thing again."

I am surprised to hear her say this. She picked up all the tricks much better than I did when I started and I had always thought of gymnastics as more painful than trapeze. Why is Christa the one to give up?

Meghan says, "Why do people start doing yoga? It begins when we yearn to strike a beautiful pose."

Friends in Scotland warned me about New York before I came for my first visit. I was told to be on the lookout for the pickpockets, junkies, murderers, and rapists who lurked in every corner of the city.

The first week I spent in New York I was constantly on edge. And, in fact, most of the worst incidents that have ever happened to me in New York came during that first week. I saw a road-rage fistfight in Hell's Kitchen between a taxi driver and a truck driver. A man masturbated in front of me outside my hostel window. Everything felt large and overwhelming; people on the streets seemed rude and aggressive. I had no idea how I could live being that fearful every day. But after the first week, I was smitten with New York and made up my mind that I wanted to stay. "That city makes me feel so alive," I'd say to people when I got home to Edinburgh.

The same thing has happened with trapeze. I love this thing I am doing, enormously, though I am unsure how to cope with the fear. As with New York, over time the fear has subsided.

Still, sometimes, the fear inflates to the point of being cartoonlike. For example, when I am in Knee Hang I always imagine I am going to fall and split my head open. This is almost impossible considering that the Aerialist is spotting me and that there are mats underneath the trapeze, but these facts don't help. Later, when I think about how absurd my thoughts are, I realize that what I really have to fear is my overactive imagination.

I have been seeing circus apparatus everywhere lately—the metal handrail on the subway car is a trapeze bar. The pillar in the middle of the room at my work is a Chinese pole for climbing. Walls are for handstands. Pipes attached to the ceiling are rigging for trapezes. Low fences are for walking the tight wire.

The contortionist, Irena Naumenko, says in an interview that, like me, she is obsessed with her training. Sometimes she wakes up in the morning and her foot is touching her head.

As I walk to trapeze class it is snowing heavily and my hair gets wet. It must be love if I'm prepared to walk to class on a cold snowy night like this.

I feel like a teenager with a silly crush. At work when I am bored or stressed, I simply have to notice the calluses on my hands and I smile. At night I dream that I'm hauling myself into a Pike on the bar, two hands grasping the bar, my body folded at the hip, my nose pressing to my belly. Sometimes I dream that people are standing on my shoulders.

My father used to work in an office. He was a buyer for an electronics company. He often came home in an irritable mood, looking dazed and weary. When I was eight years old, he was laid off and couldn't find work for three years. He applied for every job imaginable: office cleaning, office assistant, shop assistant, paperboy. Frequently, he was told he was too old, or overqualified, or underqualified.

My father needed a release from the pressures of life. He liked making and fixing things. He renovated the bathroom when I was a little girl, covering the walls with varnished oak planks. He built and installed a shower and new faucets in the sink. He built closets in my room and once when I broke the radiator because I was pulling on it while doing squats, my father didn't mind. It was something for him to fix.

In a village called Igloolik in the Canadian Arctic, an acrobat teaches circus skills to the children, in an attempt to lower the suicide rate among young people.

People are always asking me whether I'm scared of what

would happen if I fell from a trapeze. I am more scared about what would happen if I gave it up.

"Everyone loves something," says Meghan to the yoga class, "even if it's just tacos. But our passions can also be overwhelming and frightening."

I start doing daredevil things that I imagine an aerialist would do. I book a last-minute trip to New Orleans with Christa for Halloween. I pierce the top of my ear. I have a tattoo of a trapeze artist in a One-Knee Hang etched on my thigh. Printed on the cover of my notebook is a quote from Eleanor Roosevelt: "Do one thing every day that scares you."

The Aerialist drops from sitting and catches herself in an Ankle Hang.

The Aerialist drops from standing and catches herself in an Ankle Hang.

The Aerialist drops from Jezebel and catches herself in an Ankle Hang.

The Aerialist drops from standing and catches herself in a Foot Hang.

The Aerialist drops from sitting and catches herself in an Angel.

Each time the Aerialist drops, I jump. I am sure that she will sustain a painful injury, or kill herself.

The Aerialist hangs a trapeze with a low bar. It is so close to the ground that when she does a Front Balance, the ropes stretch and the bar touches the floor. My father tries to step on the bar after her but trips and belly-flops to the floor.

The Aerialist says she wants us to work on the ropes. She demonstrates, flipping up into a Pike, holding on with her hands halfway up the ropes. She comes back down; then, gripping the bar with her arms, tucks her knees to her chest. "If you can hold this for fifteen seconds," she says, "you'll be ready to do tricks on the ropes."

When it's my turn, I try to hold the position but I can't stay there for more than five seconds. Coming off, I hit my foot on the bar. Despite being close to the ground, the low bar feels more dangerous to me than the high bars, perhaps because I'm not used to working on it, or because it looks deceptively easy.

People have been known to drown in the bath.

I tell the flight attendant I have just met that I consider her very brave. Every time I fly in an airplane, I think I'm going to die. It doesn't seem natural that this large piece of machinery should be in the air.

For a long time, whenever I took a plane journey anywhere I'd let myself eat whatever I wanted—cupcakes, chocolate, café mochas—because I believed it would be my last meal. I once took a few flying trapeze lessons to feel the difference between fixed and flying trapeze. I had the same nervous feeling I did before going on a plane trip. I ate two cupcakes before I went in. I was convinced I was going to die.

"But the pilots are so well-trained," this flight attendant

says. "They are taught to deal with every possible emergency. Airplane crashes are so rare. Think about the maniacs who drive cars and how little training they've had. Think about the number of road accidents you've seen."

"But when I'm in an airplane, I feel so out of control. I cannot leave the aircraft until I arrive at my destination. If something were to happen to the plane I couldn't take control of the wheel or jump out of the plane."

"Were the office workers in the Twin Towers in control?" she asks. "If someone robs you at gunpoint, are you in control? Were you in control when you were born? Often when we think we are 'safe' or 'in control,' it's just an illusion."

"When you were a little girl you'd never let me leave the room," my mother is saying, "You wanted me by your side all the time. When I left you in the crèche to go to yoga, you screamed and cried. I felt so guilty. You were so unsure of yourself. Your brother on the other hand was so bold. Nothing scared him. He was always running away from me."

My mother is often commenting on how different my brother and I are. "I don't understand it," she says. "I brought you up the same way."

What she is saying is that we were born with our personalities. She cannot be held responsible for the way we turned out.

Most of what I know about my father I know not because he said it, but because my mother told me. The same is true of my brother. Everything I know about his life is revealed to me through my mother. I haven't spoken to him in about a year. We barely know each other.

Every Christmas my mother sticks my brother on the phone with me. He asks what I've been up to and I tell him about trapeze, yoga and what books I've been reading. But he doesn't want to know about that. He asks what pubs I go to.

Once he called me up on my birthday and started ranting about those awful war protesters in New York City and did I see them?

"Yes," I said. "I was one of them."

When I was younger, I felt that my brother was jealous of my good school report cards and grades, and, when I was older, he seemed jealous that I went to college; he thought our parents liked me better.

On the other hand I was jealous of him. I thought my brother was the golden boy. He was more sociable; everyone in our hometown seemed to like him. He was the favorite because he was the one who stayed.

When I moved to New York, my brother often asked if I missed "home." He was disappointed when I replied no. He often talked about New York as though I was on an extended vacation. He couldn't imagine that I'd built a new life for myself somewhere else. He didn't understand that my sense of "home" had been relocated.

When my father left home he seemed to forget about his mother. He hardly ever spoke to his own mother. He rarely called her or suggested a visit. It was my mother who did all that. She tried to make it clear to me that women were not supposed to stray too far from the nest.

"When your brother gets married," she used to say, "I hope I get on with his wife. It's up to the women to keep in touch. It's always the men who leave and don't bother keeping contact with their parents."

I often hide details of my life from my mother. For example, I never told her I was robbed at knifepoint, or almost raped. I do this as a way of protecting her. I know if I tell her she will stay up all night worrying about me and then call to let me know that she was up all night. So I avoid telling her things as a way of also protecting myself: I don't want to worry about my mother worrying.

My brother's relationship with her, on the other hand, is no-holds-barred. He has always been frank with her about his money troubles, car accidents, fistfights, and he often tells her intimate details of his one-night stands, even though she disapproves of them.

One time long ago, she told me, he asked her, "Have you and Dad ever tried it doggy style?"

My mother tells me my brother has been depressed and drinking a lot. Recently he was caught driving drunk for the third time and jailed overnight.

"He's still not over your father's death," my mother says.

"He needs to go to therapy," I say.

"Men don't go to therapy," my mother says.

Alarmed, I write my brother a letter. I try not to judge; in fact, I sympathize with his problem. We both lost our father. Since I have been studying trapeze I want to be closer to people and connect with them. I often find myself being more affectionate than usual, rubbing the arms of people I've just met, patting friends on the back and hugging them.

After sending the letter to my brother I hear nothing back.

My mother tells me that after five years my brother is still angry with me for leaving Scotland when I did. That is why he hasn't replied to my letter.

"She could have postponed for several months," he told her. "She left me with everything."

This is the first time I've heard my brother's side of the story. We have become so estranged from each other. I can count on one hand the number of minutes we have spoken on the phone in the last year. Now I am angry with him for not talking to me about his resentments. Why didn't he say anything at the time? I am frustrated; I want to be able to defend myself but I don't even know his phone number.

My mother once told me how thrilled my brother was when I was born. He was always pointing me out to his friends and neighbors. "That's my wee sister," he'd say proudly.

Once, the midwife came to visit, and my brother took her by the hand and excitedly guided her up the stairs to where his baby sister was sleeping.

A couple of minutes later my mother and father heard the midwife scream. My brother was trying to yank me out of the cradle by my head.

A student tells the Aerialist her calluses are sore.

"I'm grateful to have them, though," the student says. "They mark me. I used to study outdoor flying trapeze and after the summer season was over, I took six months off. But then I missed my calluses so much."

The Aerialist begins her routine eating a plate of strawberry shortcake. She glances at the trapeze, then balances the plate on her head and pulls herself up onto the trapeze. She performs a piece called "The Cake Trapeze," alternately balancing the cake on her body and eating it, while maintaining difficult positions on the trapeze. She seems to love the cake; she doesn't drop it once, and by the end of the song "Je Cherche Un Homme" she has polished it off.

I don't come from a family of healthy eaters. My father ate a bowl of canned peaches and vanilla ice cream every day. My mother never prepared fresh vegetables—rather she cooked frozen peas and Brussels sprouts. Most food items were fried or greased. In Scotland people eat deep-fat-fried Mars Bars.

When I was studying at university, my mother would always ask if I was "eating properly." What she meant was, was I eating at all? When I came to visit her, she'd insist I eat two slices of syrup cake with frosted maple icing instead of one.

The Aerialist is pairing us up to lift each other's weight on the trapeze.

"How much do you weigh?" she asks me, but I don't know the answer.

My father gets on the scales to weigh himself, then shakes his head with resignation.

Between the ages of ten and fourteen, I believed I was fat and started dieting. All I'd have for lunch was an apple and milk while other kids were eating chocolate and candy and sweet cola drinks. I worked out to aerobics videos starring Cindy Crawford, Cher or Bridget Fonda.

When I look at photographs of myself between the ages of ten and fourteen, I look skinny, though not in an unhealthy way. My body simply matured earlier than those of other girls my age. I started developing breasts when I was six and my mother was so scared by the bumps on my chest that she took me to the doctor to see if anything was seriously wrong. Was it possible for a six-year-old to have cancer? The doctor laughed and told her I'd be an early developer.

People frequently told me I was "mature for my age." I had

a swimming coach who'd shout at me and make derogatory remarks because I wouldn't dive into the water. I was afraid my head would hit the bottom. When my mother suggested that he was being too harsh on a ten-year-old, the coach looked surprised.

"I was only yelling at her because I thought she was fourteen," he said.

Later, when I was fourteen, I saw myself in the mirror after a two-hour workout. I'd spent four months trying yet another new diet and I was still not happy with my reflection. I realized that no matter what I did to "improve" my appearance, I would not be happy with it. I vowed never to go on a weight loss diet again.

A friend is asking Christa and me how often we cry. "More than once a week?" she asks jokingly. With no hesitation we answer in unison, "Yes." When I think about this I am amazed. How could I have been crying that often?

Since I've started trapeze, something has happened to my eating patterns. I'm no longer eating pizza and muffins for lunch but salads and fruit. I've become conscious of everything I'm eating. I am doing this because I want more energy. I want to feel better and more full of life so I can do more interesting tricks on the trapeze. I want to feel lighter. Something else is happening though, something I hadn't thought about before. I don't cry as often as I used to. My moods are calm and steady.

My mother is always reminding me I am from a family of men with weak hearts. All of them have died at a young age of heart attacks. I don't need to worry about cancer or strokes because there's no such family history, but she doesn't like it when I'm stressed out or afraid. "Watch your heart," she is always telling me.

I can be the same way with her. On one of her visits my mother ordered a burger with fries at McDonald's and I scolded her saying, "Why do you eat this disgusting food? You should be more careful with your heart."

She asked the vendor to Supersize her order.

At trapeze class, I try to maneuver myself into an Arrow but my hips are having a hard time rolling off the bar and when I finally come into the position, I scare myself by almost falling out of it again. And even though the Aerialist has caught me, a little voice in my head whispers, "Watch your heart."

"I keep asking myself if there was something I could have done to prevent your father's death," my mother says. "Maybe he wasn't eating healthy enough. Perhaps if I had stopped him eating peaches and ice cream he would have lived longer."

People have been commenting on the change in me. They say I am looking thin. I am supposed to take this as a compliment but I can't. I have a hard time understanding why that would be desirable in the first place. Thin, to me, is unhealthy.

It is true that since I took up trapeze I have been losing weight; I have more energy and my upper arms are more sculpted, but I'm not doing this to achieve a look.

Once in a café I sat next to a man with tight, beautiful muscles, who was discussing his no-carbs/protein supplement diet with his girlfriend. He seemed interested in his muscles not because of their potential usefulness but simply for their appearance.

The Aerialist says that circus skills are useful not only for the circus but for life.

"You can carry heavy boxes and large volumes of luggage. You can balance on ladders."

I am reading a book about the 1944 Hartford, Connecticut, circus fire. Many of the spectators were killed but all the acrobats were able to climb their way out of the tent.

I am coming to fall deeply in love with the human body and all its nuances; mine is more useful than I had ever imagined. I start reading anatomy books and then mouthing the words of the muscle groups in my body, my hands covering my forearms, elbows, triceps, shoulders, feeling the texture of my muscles, the hardness of each bone. I do this with my eyes closed, as though reading Braille.

I go to a science exhibit that compares the heart to a motor. When I think of all the electronic devices that have failed me within a couple of months of purchase, this idea scares and thrills me at the same time. Every drop of blood in the body, the exhibit notes, passes through the heart once every minute. *How do people live at all*, I wonder? In the mornings I have been waking up with a happy sense of amazement that I'm still alive.

My mother says, "Your father had a long life line on his palm. He wasn't supposed to die so young."

I once dated a man who was tall, dark, romantic and French. He put his arm around me wherever we went. He was always touching me and wanting to go everywhere with me. He was the kind of man my mother always wanted me to marry.

I didn't enjoy it. I felt claustrophobic; whenever he came near me I wanted to break into a run.

After my father died, my mother demanded more of my time. She was always asking where I'd been. Finally, in frustration with her questions, I told her I'd been on a date with a girl. She was a little shocked at first.

I was nervous telling my mother because she used to be so judgmental about other people. Once, a friend of hers had a son who was doing drugs and had to go to rehabilitation. "You have to wonder how she's bringing him up," my mother said. "You or your brother would never do anything like that." Several weeks later I was still angry with her. Then, after my father died, something in her attitude shifted. "I used to be a smug housewife," she said. "I always thought I was better than everyone else and that I had my life all sewn together—until it all fell apart."

Now she constantly tries to connect with other people. On the subway she offered candy to a girl who'd been watching her eat. "We're all people just trying to make our way in this crazy planet," she said.

After I told my mother I'd been on a date with a girl she confessed she'd had a crush on her best friend in high school.

"It was just a phase and I didn't do anything about it," she said, "but I think most people have feelings for someone of the same sex at some point in life."

Later, when I told her I was continuing to date women, she said, "Be very careful who you tell, because once you're labeled, that's it."

I have become careful of who I tell, not so much because I'm scared of a homophobic reaction but because I'm scared of carrying a fixed label. I think of the pulpy mess that remains when I try to remove labels from jam jars.

I can't tell the classic story of how I'd always hated dating men and how I much preferred being with women and how our homophobic society has held me back from acting upon my feelings, because it is not like that at all. Unsatisfied in my relationships with men, I had decided to open myself up to another possibility, but found myself running into similar problems of too much closeness.

I don't have the performer's personality. I don't enjoy attention. I like the extremes—either a big city or the middle of nowhere. These are places I can hide myself. I find myself wanting too much privacy.

I split up with my last girlfriend because, like the Frenchman, she gave me too much attention. "What have you been up to?" I asked her once after coming back from a trip.

"Waiting for you to get home," she said.

One morning she was stroking my hair as we curled up on the couch.

"When do you want to go home?" she said.

"Soon," I said. "The next hour?"

"I don't want you to go," she said, but what I needed right then was to go home and write.

Whenever I was sick as a child, my mother would make a fuss, bringing me soup, taking my temperature and giving me lozenges. Often I'd shut the door, then pretend to be asleep when she came in.

My mother wonders why my brother and I can't commit to long-term relationships.

"Is it because I smothered you?" she asks.

I don't answer.

When I was a teenager, my mother resented my studies because they took time away from her. Sometimes she'd sit in my room while I was reading a book and scribbling notes.

"Talk to me," she'd plead.

Sometimes she'd grow angry. "You're going to be a loner just like your father."

When my mother was fifteen, she trained to be a hairdresser. At hairdressing school, they told future hairdressers to read the newspaper every day so they would have something to discuss with their customers.

"There should be no silence when you're cutting someone's hair," they had instructed. "Silence is embarrassing."

When we were growing up, my mother talked incessantly. My father was a quiet man who'd jokingly taunt her with a Chas'n'Dave song, "Oh, you won't stop talking. Why don't you give it a rest? You're becoming a pest."

Whenever I was asked a question, my mother answered. People used to wonder why I was such a quiet child.

"Do you still have 'tendencies'?" my mother asks timidly, and "When you're in a relationship with a woman, how do you decide who is dominant and who is submissive?"

Her questions vex me. I've been dating women in part because I wanted to get away from those stereotypes. I was looking for a relationship that was more dynamic and I thought I could find it with a woman.

"I don't think of relationships in terms of who is dominant and submissive," I say to my mother.

"But you usually find in relationships that one is more dominant than the other," my mother insists.

I could never tell who was dominant in my mother and

father's relationship. My mother often talked as though my father were dominant but to me he was the submissive one. Just because he went out and earned money it didn't mean he got a say in how the household was run.

He was passive, for example, about his children's upbringing. My mother would be chastising my brother for some bad behavior or other and in exasperation would say to my father, "Tony, talk to him."

Barely glancing up from the TV my father would say, "Don't talk to your mother that way," and then go back to watching sports.

My mother and I are walking around the Sirens Festival on Coney Island. "Dad's Pregnant!" an ad for the Sea World announces, showing a picture of a pregnant male seahorse.

On stage a drag king is impersonating various famous black men. At the end of her skit she whips off her costume to reveal a bikini. "Oh, it's a woman. It's a woman!" my mother says, shocked and fascinated.

Later, there is a strange act involving someone dressed as a pig and someone else dressed head-to-toe as a cow.

"Which one is the man and which one is the woman?" my mother whispers in my ear as though I have some special radar.

An ex-boyfriend of mine once accused me of being "too masculine" for him. "Would it hurt you to wear lipstick once in a while?" he asked.

The curtain is being raised. First I see the bottom of a skirt. The curtain inches higher to reveal a pair of muscular arms throwing a ball. As it rises even further, we see that the person wearing the skirt is Rich. He turns to face the audience, feigns embarrassment and runs off stage.

My mother invests so much in romance. Whenever she calls, one of her first questions is, "Any romance to report?" When my brother brought girls home, my mother would always be excited, getting to know the new girlfriend, making her welcome, always wondering if she would be The One. She would invite the girlfriend to our compulsory family Sunday dinners. Then several months later there would be a breakup and my mother would find herself disappointed once again. She would get upset, as though the girl had broken up with her, too. At the end of each of my brother's romances she would be frightened of an unwanted pregnancy on top of everything else. This fear was so ingrained in her that once, when I called to tell her I'd split up with my girlfriend, she responded automatically, "She's not pregnant, is she?"

Knowing how to do a trick includes knowing how to catch yourself if you fall. I still get nervous letting go of my arms in Jezebel.

"How can you possibly fall out of this?" the Aerialist asks. "Look at how good your lock is."

Even though I do feel secure and locked in, I can't let go of my worst fears. Tito Gaona, the famous flying trapeze artist, used to dream that his arms would snap off when he was caught during a quadruple somersault. So when I'm learning a new trick, I keep asking myself, "How can you possibly fall?" I feel more comfortable with tricks once I know the escape routes. Now, learning the Front Balance, I ask the Aerialist what would happen if I fell. She has answers for everything.

"If you fall forwards, fold in half. If you fall backwards, straddle your legs so you fall into a Catcher's Lock."

She asks if I'm getting frustrated with trapeze.

"I'm always frustrated with it," I tell her.

The other day, Christa pointed out I used the word "trapped" a lot.

My mother seemed to enjoy my father's dependence on her. When I was seventeen my mother went on vacation with some friends; it was her first trip without my father. "Do his ironing while I'm gone, will you?" she said.

"I'm not doing his ironing," I said. "He's a big boy. He can figure it out himself."

"Men are useless," my mother said. "You'll soon learn."

But when my mother came back she was shocked to find my father was not only doing his ironing; he was doing *my* ironing.

"She's scary," my father jokingly whispered to my mother, pointing at me with pride.

My mother complains that my brother is always getting her to do his laundry, his ironing, clean his apartment and loan him money.

"Stop doing it, then," I say.

But my mother continues to complain about it as though she had no choice.

My father lived with his mother until he got married. He knew nothing about independence or taking care of himself. For my mother, telling me that he didn't marry until he was thirty-two is a way of giving me hope. Meaningful relationships, she is letting me know, can be started at any age.

My mother would notice that his driver's license had expired a year earlier, or that he'd forgotten to cash his paycheck. He would say, "Oh, my mother always took care of that." After he died, she confessed, "I'm glad your father died first. I don't think he could have taken care of himself."

I am telling Meghan that my mother thinks it is ridiculous that I am studying trapeze.

"Why?" Meghan asks.

I pause for a moment, not sure of the answer myself. Isn't it self-evident?

"It's because I wasn't physically active when I was younger," I reply. "And I was a bit of a wuss."

"That's so mean," Meghan says. We are at the end of trapeze class and Meghan is pulling on her boots.

When I think back to the conversation with my mother, I realize that she wasn't laughing at all. It was really half in awe, half with pleasure that she had exclaimed, "What a girl!" It was me who'd put the ridicule in her voice. I was the one mocking myself.

My mother had a yearning to fix things when she was a little girl but instead she broke everything. Once, the television broke down, and, instead of waiting for the repairman my mother, the eight-year-old, decided to take it upon herself to fix it. As she was tinkering, it blew up. This was in the fifties when televisions were a rare and expensive commodity.

When she was five, food items were still being rationed in the U.K. Once, while her mother was talking to the deliveryman, my mother cracked all the eggs open on the floor and mixed them with the flour and milk. Her mother was furious.

"What were you thinking, making this gooey mess on the floor with our rations?" she demanded. "This is all we have for the week."

"I wanted to bake a cake," my mother said.

While on vacation in New Mexico, I meet a psychic.

"You're worried about someone," she says, revealing the obvious. I tell her about my mother who is suffering from M.S. and lupus.

"Those are auto-immune diseases. It's the body attacking itself. You say that she was diagnosed shortly after your father died. She's subconsciously trying to kill herself."

I change the subject. Part of me is offended that she would say such a thing about my mother but she is also addressing a long-held fear of mine—I'm always worried that my mother is trying to kill herself off and that I'll lose her suddenly the way I lost my dad. My mother used to tell me when we were growing up that if my father died she could not continue to live. She often points out that my Uncle John died of a heart attack several months after his wife's death.

"He died of a broken heart," she said.

Shortly after my father's death, my mother took up smoking. I keep scolding her for doing such a stupid thing. When she talks to me on the phone I can hear the long exhalations of cigarette smoke.

"Don't talk to me while you're smoking," I say, both angry and frightened. Is she trying to destroy herself?

Whenever my mother used to send me things from Scotland, I could always smell home on the packages. Now they smell of home and cigarette smoke.

Because I live in New York, I am always comparing myself to other people my age who are more "successful" than I am. Most often, I think about published authors or circus aerialists who can perform tricks I may never be able to do.

One night, I tell my mother I feel "stuck." That I'm doing the same thing I've been doing for the last four years.

"Not at all," she says. "You're doing amazing things. Look at my little life. I live in this little town, I've been a hairdresser since I was fourteen, I don't have any of the opportunities you have, and I'm sick."

Saying all this, she sounds angry and resentful, which is unusual for her. When I was younger she was constantly telling me she wouldn't have her life any other way.

The Aerialist is performing on the aerial silks with Rich, who is just my height. He's svelte for a man, with leg extensions most dancers would kill for. In their act the Aerialist does most of the lifting, which causes the audience to gasp and shake their heads. How could a woman lift a man? These aerialists must also be illusionists.

But this aerialist often tells me that lifting someone is not so much about strength as knowing how to use your body.

She talks about the kinship between circus and radical politics. "I think the amazing thing about circus," she says, "is that there's a safety zone for the audience. When anyone thinks of the circus they think of some alternate reality that isn't their own."

The Aerialist is saying. "When men are around they're always trying to do everything for you. You try to spot someone or lift someone and the men jump in and say 'I'll do it.' You just can't get strong that way. You have to do these things for yourself.

"You know women are just as tough and daring as men. If you ever look at a circus history book they always make a big deal out of the achievements of Tito Gaona and the Vazquez brothers but the fact of the matter is the first person to do the triple on a flying trapeze was a teenage girl."

When I was a teenager, my school finally decided to let women play on the football team. The one woman who dared to sign up was ridiculed daily. "It's not a woman's sport. She won't be able to keep up," locals often complained.

But in spite of them, she did.

I work in an all-male office. Men are always trying to lift boxes for me. "How am I supposed to get stronger if I don't lift anything?" I am always protesting.

One man got upset when I was changing a light bulb. "I live alone," I said. "Who do you think changes the light bulbs for me?"

One day a young woman stepped into "the Cage," an outdoor basketball court near where I work, known for rough play, and the guys treated her like a man. "Coming out here is how I get better," she said. "So if a guy's not going to play me hard, I'd rather not even play."

My father used to try and pick playful physical fights with me when he was younger. I think, at first, it made him feel tough until I started to develop powerful kicks that I'd deliver to his knee. My father would often come away from the "fight" holding his leg and squealing with pain.

The Aerialist has called in sick today. Rich is in her place. The idea of having a different teacher discombobulates me. Trapeze requires so much trust, especially when a novice like me is involved.

Today, I've been thinking about why I like trapeze so much.

I used to do Egyptian dance, but I didn't go to class regularly and didn't practice the moves very often. I picked it up so easily I didn't feel I had to work at it and thus my passion was never terribly stimulated. But trapeze is different. It's precisely because it's difficult that I get excited and want to work hard.

Rich asks me to do ten Ankle Beats but I can't. I am scared he won't be able to do anything if I fall. It took me a while to trust the Aerialist, too.

"Good," he says, softly, as I come down but I'm annoyed with myself.

My father seems put out, as well. He's examining the trapeze closest to the bathroom. When I approach him, he says, "This thing is crooked."

My mother once told me my father was full of regrets. When he was a teenager he was told he was so bright he could get a scholarship to go to a boarding school and probably even college but he said he didn't want to leave his friends or the familiarity of his old school. About ten years later he started to regret his decision, wishing he could have a job that demanded more of his brain and that paid more money so he didn't have to struggle with the bills.

My mother told me that when I got into college, I was living my father's dreams for him.

My father's last job was as a bus tour guide in Edinburgh, and he was fascinated by its history. He used to drive my brother and me around Charlotte Square four or five times, quizzing us on the facts.

"And who was born in the house on our left?"

"Alexander Graham Bell," my brother and I would recite.

"And what did he invent?" my father would ask.

"The telephone."

My mother told me she thought my father would never have visited me in New York. I think that's true. He often said he didn't like traveling or going to built-up cities. "He was a content man," my mother says.

When I first moved to New York I went on lots of walking tours, but found I was hopeless at retaining facts about the city. Instead I make up little personal tours for my father.

"On my left is the Poetry Project at St. Mark's where I go

to readings. And coming up on our right is where the Twin Towers used to be. Up ahead is a coffee shop that Christa and I frequent and on our left is the studio where I learn trapeze." Sometimes my father appears by my side and looks fascinated.

I am hanging from the bar by both knees trying to get into One-Knee Hang but I can't. Right now it feels impossible.

"You need to be okay with where you're at," the Aerialist says. "You know some people would be ecstatic if they could just touch their toes."

My father is watching me in Knee Hang as though he were wishing he were able to do it, too.

I have seen the Aerialist's circus show six times now. The fifth time, I stopped looking at the acrobatic feats and started watching the shadows on the tent wall, the lighting person, the technicians and the riggers, and I would wonder what equipment they were carrying up the steps.

I watched the hooded figures backstage and tried to guess which performers were hooded and what they were about to perform. I watched them getting ready, taking their cue. I noticed subtle mistakes and could see from their breathing how exhausted and sometimes stiff they were. The backs of one performer's shoes were scuffed.

My father used to take me to the circus but I didn't enjoy seeing the wild animals perform. After the show, I remembered seeing a lion being carted off in its cage, head resting on its paws, looking miserable.

At this show, my father is sitting next to me eating popcorn. He doesn't like popcorn but there isn't anything else to eat at the kiosk. In my ear he mutters, "What's this all about? I don't understand it. That woman can't sing—she's shrieking the words to the song—and why is that man wearing a dress? He looks like a poofter."

He is saying this to wind me up. I hear him slap his thighs a couple of times and laugh. He doesn't want to admit it but, secretly, he is enjoying it.

When the juggler comes on, my father points and says, "He's good."

"He's not as exciting as the aerialists," I say. "Nobody ever died from juggling."

I am Rock Hudson going for a walk, inspired by Thoreau's essay on walking. Along the way I meet the Aerialist's grandmother. She wants to teach me how to make lasagna. A strapping man like me should eat lots of lasagna.

We are at the grandmother's house when the Aerialist appears. She looks like Botticelli's Venus, perfect and shapely, hair much longer than usual.

"She's not what you think, you know," the grandmother says. I am not what she thinks either. I am a woman posing as Rock Hudson.

"You've got to use lots of tomato and mozzarella," the grandmother is instructing me. The lasagna is a big yellow red mushy pulp like muscles. It tastes better than it looks.

"Dance with her," the grandmother says.

So I dance with the Aerialist. I keep thinking the Aerialist will realize at some point that I am a woman and not Rock Hudson. I am holding her as though she is a man. The Aerialist looks happy; she hasn't noticed and she doesn't care. She gazes lovingly at me the way Doris Day stares at Rock Hudson.

One night at the supermarket I see the Aerialist, wearing a bandana, ripped jeans and a plain white T-shirt, and carrying a cloth bag. She is examining some carrots. She looks so ordinary; no one would ever suspect her of being an aerialist. But I don't know what else I had expected.

"You idealize the Aerialist," Christa says. " And you have a crush on her, I can tell, because you're always getting crushes on people you think are unattainable. It's your way of avoiding relationships."

I get to trapeze class early just in time to catch the Aerialist in training with the director of her performing troupe.

She is in Toe Hangs, attempting to take one foot off the bar. The director is spotting her.

"My skin feels like it's coming off!" she cries. She breathes heavily, her face going red.

"Try it one more time," the director says, her hands hovering around the Aerialist's hips.

The Aerialist takes a big breath in and tries to take her foot off the bar. It lifts off a couple of inches away from the bar. The Aerialist breathes out then puts her foot back on.

"Sorry," she says to the director. The director shakes her head.

"It'll take a while," she says.

The Aerialist comes off the bar and walks past me muttering, "Shit!"

After I left home my father never called me for a chat. It was always my mother who'd call and then stick the phone up to my father's ear.

"Eh-heh?" he'd say, sounding awkward.

Then he'd ask if everything was all right. Often, in desperation for things to say, he'd ask what I'd had for lunch to which I'd frequently reply, "I can't remember." Then my mother would get back on the phone.

I don't know much about my father's childhood, simply that he was born in north London and that his mother's name was Louisa. The only reason I know this is because my middle name is Louise after her, except that, according to my mother, my father remembered his own mother's name wrong. My middle name should be Louisa.

My father told only one story of his childhood and he told it over and over again. During the Second World War, when he was four, an air raid siren went off in the middle of the night, and his family had to evacuate and stay in the air raid shelter; however, when they reached the bottom, Uncle Pat realized he had left his teddy bear, Brutus, behind. Life was not worth living without Brutus, so he went back to his room to retrieve the bear. Uncle Pat came running back into the shelter all in a panic, and, as he reached the door, a bomb went off. He got such a fright he jumped up and hit his head on the ceiling.

My father used to tell this story with such hilarity. His brother banging his head was the punch line.

When I was growing up my father and I used to take long walks together and never say a word. I felt like no one understood the joy of being alone except the two of us. It wasn't that we didn't have anything to say to each other. It was just that we enjoyed nothing better than being alone with another person.

Our relationship shifted once I went to college. I wanted more from him. He'd often use humor to avoid letting anyone know what was really going on with him. I felt like I didn't know him well. When I was going to school in Edinburgh, he used to pick me up on Christmas day to drive me back to Livingston. Most of the one-hour journey would be wordless; we'd simply listen to music on the radio. It didn't matter how long we'd have gone without seeing each other—weeks or months—we really had very little to say.

Every year, it was traditional for us to discuss how we could get my mother's sister, who neither of us liked very much, off the phone. This topic would engage us for several minutes. Often, he would say, "Sex. Just talk about sex. That'll get her off the phone pretty quickly." Afterwards he would imitate a female voice, "We don't talk about these things in England." Once that topic of conversation was finished, the car would go quiet again. I'd bite my lip and turn up the radio.

Christa comments that in trapeze shows the woman is often portrayed as dominant, but I think it's more than that. Trapeze seems to attract independent women and playing a dominant role is a way to express that power.

When I was a teenager, my mother would often accuse me of being selfish; she told me if I kept up such behavior I'd be alone for the rest of my life. At the time, this sounded like a curse. The possibility of not having a life partner used to fill me with dread; now I'm comfortable being alone and the idea doesn't scare me anymore.

"Trapeze can be a selfish pursuit, like writing," the Aerialist says.

At the circus show, the Aerialist, gliding in the air, ends her solo act by swooping down onto a pool, dipping her feet into the water and spraying it on the acrobats. On the stage the acrobats are playing in the simulated rain.

To the people I grew up with in a working-class town an hour from Edinburgh, I was something of an oddity. I read books that didn't have pictures; I had English parents; I used "big words" in my conversation; I was quiet; I liked to write. People thought I was weird and I began to identify myself that way.

When I got to college I found myself an outsider in another way. Almost everyone there had a mother or father who was a lawyer or a professor or a scientist. They had been brought up reading Shakespeare and Dickens and watching Truffaut's films and Kieslowski's *Three Colors* trilogy, things I was just starting to discover.

I have noticed circus people are frequently regarded as outsiders. I wonder if that's why, among them, I feel a sense of belonging.

My mother said my father had died the way he wanted to. No fuss, no pain, no long drawn-out illness, no emotional deathbed scene. He died the way I want to die.

The Aerialist decides I should practice letting go of my arms in Jezebel. We repeat the trick about twenty times, and by the time I'm done drilling it, I'm so bored with it I don't even think when I let go. My father, inspired by my progress, tries to touch his toes again. I am afraid he will get stuck there. He has a habit of doing things like that.

Once, the family went walking on Cramond beach in Scotland. My father's hip was hurting and he decided to sit on a rock while we walked around the beach. He didn't realize the tide was coming in and when we came back for him, he couldn't come down off the rock without getting soaked waist-deep.

"Tell me a story," I used to beg my mother every night before I went to bed. I'd often exhaust her with my love of hearing tales. Quite frequently she'd tell me the story of how she was "through with men" when she met my father at a jazz club. He asked her to dance with him eight times before she finally said yes. As soon as he took her in his arms she knew he was The One. I liked to hear the tale over and over again. It sounded like Cinderella.

My mother was exasperated with my love of books. I couldn't seem to read enough; she didn't know what to suggest. Frequently she'd give me the romance novels she'd been reading. I devoured those. Every novel was the same. The men were tall, overpowering, strong, dark with throbbing manhoods; the women blonde, delicate, and slim. They always lived happily ever after. I began to imagine this was how all relationships were supposed to be. It wasn't until much later in life I realized that these tales were a setup for disappointment.

My mother frequently expresses unease about being single again. In my hometown the first question most people ask is, "Got a boyfriend?" or "Are you married?" If the answer to the question is "No," the frequent reaction of the asker is pity or suspicion.

When I moved to New York I met an Englishwoman at a party who asked, "Did you leave a boyfriend behind in Scotland?"

"No," I replied, slightly irritated.

There was a slight pause. "Girlfriend?" she asked.

Now the question really bothered me. Why did I have to be coupled off?

The Aerialist is trying to get me to bring one knee off the bar for the One-Knee Hang but the back of my knee will not peel away from the bar.

"You have a 'letting go' issue," the Aerialist jokes.

I used to believe my mother when she said she and my father had the perfect marriage, but as I got older I started to realize there were some things wrong. She would complain that my father didn't talk to her or help around the house. She'd often accuse him of not being involved in our upbringing. My father would storm off to the living room and blank her out by watching television.

My mother told me my brother said he wanted a relationship just like my mother and father's. He wanted a woman who would stay home and bring up the children just like my mother did. Even my mother thinks his expectations are unrealistic for the times.

"You're going to have a hard time finding what you're looking for in a relationship because you like unconventional people," an astrologer says to me. "You also like your freedom but need a deep connection. Most people want one or the other but you need both."

It occurs to me that my own expectations of relationships are as unrealistic as my brother's. Often, I subject the relationship to doom before it has even begun. I worry that I will delude myself into thinking I'm happy. I imagine how I will have less space and freedom and how this will automatically lead to arguments. All I can think about is the messy breakup. At other times, I am at the other end of the spectrum. I come to expect so much from romance that any relationship turns out to be a disappointment.

What I am really grappling with is the ability to be present.

When I am upside down on a trapeze I am aware of the danger and I am so focused I can't think about anything else like what's for dinner or what time I'm going to get home or relive an argument from that day. All I can think about is what I'm doing at that moment.

Christa and I always joke that we prefer fantasy relationships to real relationships, like the dolls you can buy at Coney Island called "Grow Your Own Girlfriend" or "Grow Your Own Boyfriend." In a fantasy relationship no one will argue with you or ask you what time you're getting home at night or grow annoyed at bad habits. My mother says that in her late teens when she was dating someone she thought she would marry, she was in love with being in love. And that's why she stayed for so long with this man who made her so unhappy.

I am aware that since my father's death I have come to idolize him. Sometimes I feel sad that I enjoy the memory of him more than I enjoyed him when he was actually alive.

My mother says of our relationship, "We get along so well now," but what she leaves out is that we get along so well now because I live thousands of miles away.

"Your father wasn't a romantic man," my mother is telling me. "When we were courting I used to ask him to whisper something romantic in my ear and he always said 'Charlie George' who was the Arsenal goalkeeper at the time."

There is a bruise between my armpit and elbow as big as a tennis ball and black as night. Christa squirms when I show her. "I hope the bruises are worth it," she says to me. They are.

Christa is showing me a mark on her shin that she picked up because her husband was tossing and turning in the bed and accidentally kicked her. He often does that she complains. She grumbles about his mood swings, tells me he has the male version of PMS, and says she's tired of him interrupting her writing all the time because he wants to talk.

"You're so lucky to be single," she says to me but, in fact, she is always telling me how much she loves her husband.

I always wish I could ask people about their relationships, *are the bruises worth it?*

Before I moved to New York I would often show my mother books with pictures of New York in them. "I'm so in love with this city," I'd say.

"You can't fall in love with a city. You have to fall in love with a person," my mother would reply.

"Whenever I become involved in a relationship," I tell Christa, "I have a hard time figuring out when I should leave the relationship and when I just need to work at it. I know relationships require work."

"You leave when you stop loving that person," says Christa.

Later I begin telling her about my frustration with trapeze. "I don't feel like I'm progressing. I still can't do One-Knee Hang without a spot. After several months of trying Back Balance it's not coming along. I want to quit."

Christa laughs. "Don't be ridiculous; you're never going to quit. I never see you anymore because you're always at trapeze class. I think you'd marry a trapeze if such a thing were possible."

I am telling a friend about another friend, divorced just recently, who wants to marry the new person she is in love with.

"That's lame. Maybe she shouldn't get married again. I would never do something like that."

How could she know? I ask her. We're all capable of doing things we've never imagined. The only sure thing I know about myself is that I am subject to change.

"Why do you like trapeze so much?" I ask the Aerialist.
"I like that so many possibilities exist within the confines of such a small space," she replies.

As she teaches her yoga class, Meghan says, "I read a great definition of 'letting go.' It's 'Love mixed with space.'"

I am reading about a fire-eater who describes how fire fascinates her. In the name of art, she has received third-degree burns, singed her hair, gone to hospital twice, and burned a favorite dress; her mouth stinks of petroleum. She says she is intrigued by the way the body heals. Thoroughly aware of the dangers her profession entails, she's got plenty of horror stories that would put anyone off, but she can't give up.

"I love watching fire. It's so beautiful."

It is not the fire in her photograph that I find beautiful. It's her, and the way she looks at the fire and touches the fire. I can't imagine doing what she does. I don't love fire enough to accept the risks.

Later she says that she can't imagine wanting to be a trapeze artist. It's too dangerous for her.

I go to a trapeze workshop at a different studio for a day. The teacher begins the class by asking if any of us have a history of injuries or are presently hurt. If so, how were the injuries acquired. Some people in the class, like me, have very little trapeze experience; others have worked for years in the circus. Yet none has had a mishap that can be attributed to the circus. More often, everyday things like bending down to pick up a package cause trouble. The Aerialist herself has a large gash in her thumb; she cut herself slicing a bagel.

When I was twenty and visiting New York for the first time, I was concerned with being "nice." I took a bus all the way from New York to North Carolina and got stuck next to a man who kept asking me to marry him, or hold his hand. He kept asking to sing me a lullaby. I was too nice and too scared to tell him to get lost, so he harassed me for the whole ten-hour ride; I was miserable.

Now I take a bus from New York to Philadelphia. The bus is almost empty and a young man puts his bag next to me. "I'm going to sit next to you," he says.

"No," I say, "I'll move elsewhere if you want this seat but I want to sit alone and read."

The young man tries to guilt-trip me. "I understand; you don't want to be bothered by *some guy*."

"No, I don't," I say without a trace of malice. I don't feel guilty as I might have done in the past. I am just being honest about what I want.

After I was almost raped, then mugged, I became neurotic about traveling late at night. I took taxis everywhere, even for just a few blocks. I made my friends call me as soon as they got home and I did the same. I always cautioned people to be careful. I became like my mother.

Before class starts, the Aerialist asks us to warm up by each lifting a partner backwards and over the curve of our backs, then holding them in that position for some time. A stocky guy standing next to me who looks as though he weighs two hundred pounds asks to partner with me. Out of politeness I say yes, but I'm scared I'll drop him. I may look like the biggest woman in the class, but I'm not the strongest.

The Aerialist sees I've partnered up with the man and watches me with a slight look of amusement as I take his wrists in my hands and wriggle my butt under his to lift him up onto my back. To my surprise, his legs lift off the floor and I hold him for several minutes until he is ready to come down.

At night, I walk out into the cold. Twenty feet away three men in a group are walking toward me. For once, I don't cross the street. I stay on the same path and as I walk by them, I smile.

I went to a self-defense class shortly after the attempted rape. The instructor said, "People don't love themselves enough. If your loved one were being attacked you'd go after them like a bear but if you were the one being attacked you'd probably not put enough energy into defending yourself."

I read an anecdote somewhere about Roman Polanski. He said, "It's very hard, you know, to knock someone out. See this? See this here?" He lifted his hair back over his scalp to show his friend a scar. "Man tried to knock me out once when I was a kid, big guy, and he had to hit me seven times with a rock—hard—before he finally succeeded in doing so, and even then I was only out for a few moments. It's not that easy to knock someone out."

Miguel and Juan Vazquez trained for their quadruple somersault on the flying trapeze by boxing each other every day because it was good for their reflexes and because it got them used to feeling sudden body blows should they collide midair.

I think back to the time I was almost raped and how I was too scared to punch the guy because he might punch me back. The Aerialist is teaching me Knee Hang on the rope, a trick that leaves the nastiest blackest-looking bruises on my legs as though someone has been beating me up. I have been thinking this is what it must feel like to be punched. The idea of fighting back doesn't scare me anymore.

In trapeze we often ask for a "psychological spot." This means we can do the trick but we're nervous about it and would feel happier if someone were watching in case we lose our balance or our grip and fall. The psychological spot may not be able to do anything but there is something about being watched while on a trapeze that makes one feel secure. When someone is watching us, we are less likely to be sloppy. We are more attentive to what we are doing.

I am performing a solo piece in front of the class, and I realize I am being more daring than normal. It feels like angels are watching me. With all these supportive eyes on me, I am thinking, how can I possibly fall?

"Whenever I perform I want to see people's faces," the Aerialist says to me. "People are always looking at me when I perform but I rarely get to look at them. And when I do catch glimpses of them they don't always look as riveted or excited as I'd want them to be. And if I'm going to give a good show I need to see my audience likes and appreciates what I'm doing. Sometimes I wish I could audition the audience," she jokes.

In class doing Knee Beats Meghan falls, but lands well on the thick mats, tucking her head before she hits the ground. She is completely unharmed though a little shaken. It is the Aerialist who seems the most disturbed by her fall. Meghan is back up on the trapeze five minutes later, but the Aerialist is more watchful than usual.

While I do my Knee Beats she holds onto my feet.

"I know you know how to do this, but I'd feel better if I thought everyone was safe," she says. "It's just for tonight."

I don't argue. I want to protect her.

The Aerialist has more faith in me than I have in myself. I am trying to take my knee off the bar for One-Knee Hang. It is a trick I believe to be beyond me; nonetheless when it is my turn, I can see the Aerialist watching me out of the corner of her eye, hoping I will complete it.

"You never know when the miracle might happen," she says.

She tells me to imagine I'm strong. I have been working on this trick for the last year.

"Pull your ribs in," she tells me. "You need your whole body working to stay on there. Imagine you're the strongest person in the world and take your knee off."

My father is standing above me on the bar with a reassuring smile. What is he doing here? He is scared of heights. I lengthen my spine, pull my ribs in. My knee is on the edge of the bar, dangling. It is edging off the bar and I am not falling.

The Aerialist has told me to imagine I am strong, and I as I do that, I actually feel myself becoming stronger.

"Sometimes you can change a person's whole path of doing something with the tiniest adjustment in movement."

I thought she was going to say, "You can change a person's whole life."

My mother says she couldn't watch the circus when she was younger because the fierce animals made her nervous and she thought the trapeze artists were sure to die. She is often tripping and stumbling on the sidewalk going about her daily business. There is a large scar on her cheek from her most recent fall.

Even before I started taking trapeze, I would often find mysterious bruises and cuts on my body. People would ask, "How did you get that?" and I would have no memory of where the mark had come from.

There is a circus clown who slides and falls for laughs, but miraculously there's not a bruise on her.

My mother is full of self-doubt. When she first visited New York she was terrified of touring the city by herself while I went to work. On the first day, I gave her a subway map, a tourist book and a long sheet of instructions. When I left her at the station, she had a frantic look on her face. I was worried the whole day.

Later, I met her outside the Empire State Building and she was glowing. She described all the places she'd been and all the people she'd met. She was beside herself with excitement.

My mother visits again. Over dinner, she says, "I wish I had a strong man to protect me."

My father is sitting next to her, stuffing his face with ice cream. He puts down his spoon when she says this, stares at her with something like desire, then touches her hand. My mother doesn't know this.

"You don't need a man to protect you," I say. "You're

doing a good job of looking after yourself."

When we go to catch the subway there is a man playing the bongos at the bottom of the stairs, an enormous fat man wearing a thong decorated with pompoms. His belly wobbles up and down as he plays.

My mother can't stop laughing.

"What about him?" I ask, teasingly. "There's a strong man to protect you."

My mother and I are walking through Central Park where people are rollerblading, biking and running. My mother has to walk very slowly and take breaks on a park bench every fifteen minutes.

My mother tells me not to take my young body for granted. "I used to study yoga in my thirties and I could do a full Lotus in headstand."

It is distressing for me to see how much she has declined. While her body has been deteriorating, I have been getting stronger. "It's amazing what other people can do with their bodies," she says. "When I was first struck with the M.S. and I had trouble walking I used to get so envious and frustrated, but now I've come to accept my limitations and I'm working with the illness."

My mother is full of the belief that I am going to do very well in life. And when I do become rich and famous, I'll buy her a holiday home in a hot country like Spain and take her sailing on my personal yacht.

"It may not happen for another ten or twenty years," she says. "I may even be eighty by the time you become rich and famous, but that's okay because I can wait until then."

I feel relieved: my mother has promised to live until she's eighty.

Every Christmas Eve at midnight, my mother would make us leave a glass of sherry and a mince pie out for "Santa." Later I realized that the offerings increased every year. One year, we had to leave two glasses of sherry for "Santa" and "his reindeer." The next year, we had to leave the whole bottle of sherry so "Santa" could help himself. My mother would show us pictures of "Santa Claus" throwing my father over his lap and spanking him with a slipper for being a naughty boy. When I grew older, I realized "Santa Claus" was my uncle.

My mother sends me a photograph of myself taken when I am six years old. I'm dressed as a ballerina in a leotard. One arm is pointing diagonally upwards, one arm pointing diagonally downwards; my right foot is pointing to the side and stretching in an arabesque.

Christa says to me, "You look like a future trapeze artist in this photo."

"Do you remember when you were little and you fell over doing a handstand?" my mother asks.

"I couldn't do handstands when I was younger," I tell her.

"Yes, you could," she says. "You fell and scraped your knee quite badly and you banged your mouth. You were really scared and cried for hours afterwards. You wouldn't do another handstand after that."

I have no recollection of this and I am not sure whose memory is faulty.

Christa's father-in-law died several years ago. "My husband is still depressed," she says. "I don't know how you get over a thing like that."

My own coping mechanisms have changed. Instead of looking for my father by imagining him in the room with me, I've also started to see his personality in other people, everywhere.

Meghan comes roaring up behind me, taps me on the back and teasingly says, "You cheated on the last pushup." The class laughs and I laugh at myself. My father is sitting off to the side, pouting, as though Meghan had just stolen his line.

My mother keeps telling me I look like my dad.

Christa sits in on a class and watches me work. "You were amazing," she says. "I could never do some of that stuff. Those things you call Monkey Rolls look so difficult."

"But you can walk on your hands and do freestanding handstands without a wall," I reply. "You can do back flips and handstand tucks. I can't do any of the acrobatic stuff you can. I'm pretty useless."

We catch each other's eyes and laugh. We could go on like this forever.

Meghan says, "Don't be jealous of what other people have got. Want what you have."

Because New York is full of characters doing wild and different things, I imagine myself to be a dull person. When I think about what success means to me, I don't think about money or getting a mortgage or getting married, I think about whether my life is interesting, or, in other words, would it make a good story? Would it be a story people would be interested in reading?

Recently, when I was traveling, I met a woman from a rural area in the South. We talked for a long time about each other's lives. She'd survived cancer; she'd raised chickens in the countryside; she was a retired schoolteacher. To me she was fascinating. But she was the one who said to me, "You're the most interesting person I've ever met."

I am perched on the trapeze as the Aerialist is saying, "I just wanted to tell you how much I admire you. It isn't just because you're dedicated and enthusiastic," she says. "You're patient with yourself. You don't get frustrated; you just keep working at it. And you've come a long way in a short amount of time."

The Aerialist is telling *me* how much *she* admires *me*. Now I am on the pedestal, and I'm not comfortable up here. I want to come down. I want to tell her how impatient I am and give her a list of the tricks I still can't do. I am clumsy, inflexible, and a slow learner. These are the things I like to tell myself when I get home at night. I am always beating myself up.

But the Aerialist is looking at me with such pride. I am her student and she has seen me go through so much.

"Thank you," I say to her, as I jump down nervously from the trapeze.

I don't believe in heaven, but I like the concept. Sometimes, I like to imagine what my father would do there. He'd be eating peaches and ice cream every day, smoking cigarettes, watching football; and he'd have access to all the socks and handkerchiefs he could want.

For me, heaven is full of aerialists, dangling limply from hoops, fabric silks and trapeze bars. In heaven, I will be strong and supple.

Sometimes, when I go to trapeze class, I think, "This is where I want to die."

The Aerialist started out as a rigger for the circus. She used to watch with envy the shadows of trapeze artists projected on the tent walls as the artists themselves performed in front of ecstatic audiences. A coach started giving her advice, telling her what exercises to do and how to get strong. Later she became the star aerialist with that circus.

"Now it's my shadow," she says, "that is projected against the wall of the tent."

In the summer I go to an aerial dance festival in Colorado. For the first time, I get to play around on the lyra, a steel hoop with a four-foot diameter hanging from a single rope. My teacher is telling me first to stand inside the hoop, then hook my right knee over the top, then the other knee, so I am at the top of the lyra in a Knee Hang. My arms let go and the hoop swings gently around so that I get a view of the mirror on the wall across the room.

Out of the corner of my eye I notice someone in the mirror. Her hair is hanging loose and free. She seems happy, confident, and strong. Her belly is showing, her mouth is slightly open, her calves are bruised. I feel nervous for her and want to tell her to come down.

But I don't.

Acknowledgments

I'd like to thank my editor, Dick Lourie, for making many astute and wonderful suggestions which have improved the book beyond anything I could have imagined. Donna Brook offered thoughtful comments from a very early stage and went through several drafts in great detail, and the rest of the Hanging Loose team, Robert Hershon, Mark Pawlak, and our intern, Ben Chartoff, contributed criticism and enthusiasm.

The following offered helpful edits and/or encouragement: Shell Fischer; Sharon Mesmer; Taniya Sen; Joanna Fuhrman; Christine Shook; Boni Joi; Susanna Fry; Arielle Guy; Donald Breckenridge; Maria Dahvana Headley; and Carolyn Turgeon.

Thanks to Maike Schultz for providing a gorgeous cover photo, and Tanya Gagne for being the trapeze artist model.

Love to my mother, for all her enthusiasm and support.

Over the last few years I've been taught by a variety of trapeze teachers, but I'd particularly like to send heartfelt thanks to Natalie Agee for all her patience and teaching me tricks I never thought I'd pull off in a million years, and I Wang, who has been my trapeze partner for the last two years. She has never once seemed ruffled by the challenges that trapeze presents and always offered support when I needed it most. I'd also like to thank Sarah East Johnson, Diana Y. Greiner and Simone Genziuk for their inspiration.

My life has been transformed by so many teachers and yogis at the Laughing Lotus yoga studio. Special thanks to: Dana Flynn and Jasmine Tarkeshi, co-founders and directors of the studio; Eden Kellner who made me fall in love with yoga in the first place; and Edward Vilga, for being an extraordinary yoga teacher and friend. And, of course, to Belle!

I could not have completed this book without the time, space and support offered by my residency at the MacDowell Colony.

Excerpts/adaptations of *The Trapeze Diaries* have appeared in *The Best Creative Nonfiction* (W.W. Norton, 2007), *Hanging Loose* and *turntablebluelight.com*.

The Trapeze Diaries